This book belongs to:

. . . .

To my beautiful Lottie, for all the steps she's taken and all the steps to come. A.S.

*This book is dedicated to Aslom for his work with children,
and to Jaime's admiration for him. L.M.*

OXFORD
UNIVERSITY PRESS

Great Clarendon Street, Oxford OX2 6DP

Oxford University Press is a department of the University of Oxford.
It furthers the University's objective of excellence in research, scholarship,
and education by publishing worldwide in

Oxford New York

Auckland Cape Town Dar es Salaam Hong Kong Karachi
Kuala Lumpur Madrid Melbourne Mexico City Nairobi
New Delhi Shanghai Taipei Toronto

With offices in
Argentina Austria Brazil Chile Czech Republic France Greece
Guatemala Hungary Italy Japan Poland Portugal Singapore
South Korea Switzerland Thailand Turkey Ukraine Vietnam

Text copyright © Amber Stewart 2010
Illustrations copyright © Layn Marlow 2010

British Library Cataloguing in Publication Data available

ISBN: 978-0-19-275781-4 (paperback)

10 9 8 7 6 5 4 3 2 1

Printed in China

Paper used in the production of this book is a
natural, recyclable product made from wood
grown in sustainable forests. The manufacturing process
conforms to the environmental regulations of the country
of origin.

Amber Stewart & Layn Marlow

Puddle's Big Step

OXFORD
UNIVERSITY PRESS

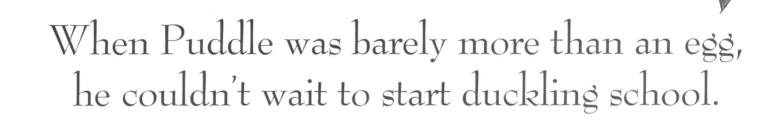

When Puddle was barely more than an egg,
he couldn't wait to start duckling school.

Every day, Puddle and his two friends, Pip and Fern, would watch the bigger ducklings waddling to and from Willow Brook Duckling School.

They looked so grown-up —
each with their own school bag . . .

and Puddle wished
to be just like them.

Then, one day, while Puddle was helping
Mummy to make his favourite biscuits,
Mummy gave him a big hug and said,
'Puddle, now *you* are big enough
to start duckling school.'

Puddle's feathers fluffed out with pride.

'Will I have my very own
school bag, Mummy?'
he asked.

'Yes you will,'
Mummy smiled.
'Your own special bag.'

But tucked up in their nest that night,
Puddle imagined his first day at school and
his little heart went pitter-patter, pitter-patter.

As he edged just that bit closer to Mummy's warm, soft feathers, Puddle knew that he'd been wrong. He *could* wait to go to duckling school . . .

he could wait until he was a very old duck indeed.

'Every new little duckling at Willow Brook
will feel wobbly today,' Mummy said kindly,
slipping Puddle's bag over his wing.

'Your first day at school
is a very big step.'

But Puddle wasn't sure he could take even

one

very

small

step.

His feet
felt stuck to
the ground.

'You'll have fun,' smiled Mummy,
as she shooed him gently along the
stepping-stones into school.
'You're my brave little duck.'

As Puddle put down his school bag, he spotted
something . . . something very familiar.

It was one of mummy's smallest, softest feathers.
She had tucked it inside to show she was never far away.

Then Puddle felt brave enough
to take his next big step . . .

and found a place to sit on the water-lily mat.
'I like your feather,' whispered the little duck beside him.

The morning went by in a flurry of . . .

matching
ladybirds . . .

counting
caterpillars . . .

and lily-pad leaping . . .

until their teacher clapped
her wings and asked them
all to settle down for lunch.

Puddle and Mummy had lunch together every day.
Suddenly, she did seem very far away.

But when Puddle took his lunch box
from his special bag, he found Mummy had
packed all his favourite nibbles . . .

and four best home-made biscuits —
one for him, one for Pip, one for Fern,
and one for a new friend, too.

After lunch, it was nap-time
under the willow tree.

Puddle peeped in his bag,
hoping that Mummy had
remembered his Cuddly . . .

and she had.

Later, all the ducklings made presents
for their mummies and daddies.

Some did
feet painting,

some made
daisy chains,

and some did
twig decorating.

At going-home time, Puddle tucked
his twig carefully into his bag, and ran
happily along the stepping-stones
for a warm, soft hug with Mummy.

Snuggled up in their nest that night,
Puddle thought about his first day at school
and his little heart went pitter-patter,
pitter-patter with excitement . . .

he couldn't wait to see
what he would do tomorrow
at duckling school.